CROSS COUNTRY

Kate Needham
Designed by Ian McNee

Illustrated by Mikki Rain
Photographs by Kit Houghton
Consultant: Juliet Mander BHSII

Series Editor: Felicity Brooks
Managing Designer: Mary Cartwright
American Editor: Peggy Porter Tierney
American Consultant: Lynn K. Anthony

Contents

WHAT IS CROSS-COUNTRY ?

Cross-country riding means riding off the roads and outside the schooling ring. It can be across fields, through woods or down country tracks with all kinds of natural obstacles and fences to tackle on the way. Whether your goal is to compete or simply ride for fun, you will need good basic riding and jumping skills.

CROSS-COUNTRY FOR FUN

Sponsored or fun rides

These non-competitive events are usually organized in aid of a charity, and are a good introduction to cross-country for you and your pony. They get you used to riding in open country with other ponies, and there are normally a few optional fences. Look for advertisements in local papers, saddlery shops or riding schools.

Hunting and mock hunting

Hunting is one of the earliest forms of cross-country riding and many of today's events stem from this sport. During a fast chase, riders have to tackle whatever obstacles they meet. These days mock hunting or drag hunting is becoming more popular. Instead of chasing a fox, a scent is laid for the hounds to follow.

COMPETITIVE CROSS-COUNTRY

Hunter trials

These events are often organized by local hunts. Originally their purpose was to train riders and horses for hunting, but nowadays they include classes for all ages and standards. The aim is to ride clear around a course of jumps built across several fields, usually within an optimum time limit.

Eventing

In one-, two-, or three-day events, the cross-country course is one of three parts of the competition. The other two are dressage and show jumping. Eventing is a thorough test of both horse and rider's fitness and stamina.

Long distance riding

Long distance riding is a competitive sport which involves riding, but not necessarily jumping, across country. Courses are usually from 80 to 120km (50 to 75 miles) long, so you and your pony have to be very fit to take part. Vets are on hand to check the ponies' health at various stages on a long distance ride.

Team chase

In this event, four riders race around a cross-country course as fast as possible. No points are lost for falls or refusals and it is the times of the first three riders home that count. Team chase is fast and competitive, so it is usually restricted to older, more experienced riders.

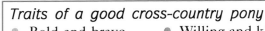

A good cross-country horse or pony needs to be brave and a bold jumper.

Traits of a good cross-country pony

- Bold and brave
- Fit and athletic
- Sound and healthy, with strong legs
- Obedient and well-trained
- Sure-footed
- Willing and kind
- Calm but not lazy
- A good, willing jumper, but also careful
- The right size and strength for you

RIDING OUTDOORS

Once you leave the relative safety of an indoor ring or enclosed arena, all kinds of factors change. Ground and weather conditions will vary and there are likely to be hills to tackle. Your pony may also be more excitable than usual, so before heading off across country, make sure you can keep control.

STAYING IN CONTROL

Most people learn to ride in an indoor ring or arena where it is easier to control a pony. Out in the open the pace is usually faster and ponies often become harder to control. If you lose control, your pony could go a long way before deciding to stop.

Tips for control

- Try to stay in complete balance with your pony at all times with light contact on his mouth.
- Shorten your reins whenever you pick up speed.
- Sit up well and be firm with your pony.
- If you do get out of control, stay calm. Panicking will make the pony go faster.
- Head toward a large hedge – make sure it is too big for him to jump.
- Head uphill – this will slow your pony down.
- Turn your pony in a circle. Make the circle smaller as he slows down.

This pony is pulling on the reins and could easily get out of control.

This rider is in control of her pony and he is listening to her aids.

YOUR POSITION

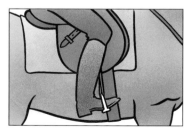

Whenever you go cross-country riding, you need to shorten your stirrups by a couple of holes. This helps you to change your position slightly.

Shorter stirrups allow you to move your weight forward easily. This helps your pony balance at faster speeds and also helps you to keep control.

To steady your pony or urge him on, sit back in the saddle to give the aids. This is the position you will need for the approach to most jumps.

COPING WITH BAD GROUND CONDITIONS

In wet weather the takeoff and landing areas of a jump can become very muddy.

Conditions that make life more difficult for your pony are hard or slippery ground or very soft ground such as deep mud or plowed soil. Hard ground can hurt your pony's legs, causing splint or tendon damage, (see pages 9 and 31) so be careful not to ride too fast or jump too much on it. If you do have to ride on hard ground, let your pony go more slowly and jump smaller fences.

Riding through heavy mud or soft ground is tiring for your pony and will slow him down. It can also cause damage to his legs. Jumping from soft or heavy ground requires a lot more effort.

Hot, dry weather usually means hard ground. Let your pony go more slowly in these conditions.

WEATHER AND MOOD

As well as influencing the ground conditions, weather can alter the mood of your pony. On a hot day he could be sleepy and lazy, while windy conditions may make him excitable and easily spooked.

On a windy day, a nervous pony will find more things to spook at than usual.

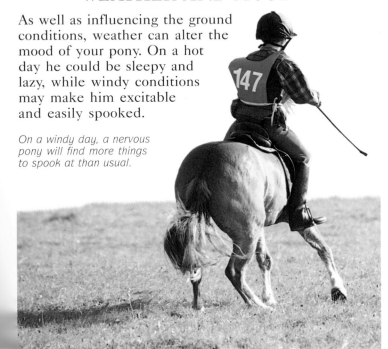

CROSS-COUNTRY COURTESY

When riding across country, you are usually on someone else's land, so it is important to respect it. You are also likely to be out with other riders, so be considerate to them too.

Points to remember
- Keep to the trail.
- If there are animals in a field, ride around them.
- Close any gates that you open.
- Approach any other riders calmly.
- If you are having trouble at a jump and someone else is close behind, let the other rider pass ahead.

HILLS AND SLOPES

Ponies bred in the mountains can be very sure-footed on the steepest of slopes, but other breeds may find hillwork quite difficult. They have to adjust their balance and pace, though you can help by altering your position slightly. Hillwork is good fitness training, but don't overdo it, as too much can put strain on your pony's legs.

RIDING UPHILL

Going up a hill is easier for your pony than going down or across it. This is because his power is in his hindquarters. It does take extra effort, though, and he will use a shorter stride. To help his balance, fold forward from the hips. This takes your weight off his hindquarters. Move your hands forward so that he can stretch his neck. Your position will depend on the slope. The steeper it is, the farther forward you need to be.

Warning

Remember to check your girth before riding up and down hills.

Attack a steep slope in a bouncy trot or canter so that your pony has plenty of impulsion.

RIDING ACROSS A SLOPE

Moving across a hill is very difficult for ponies. They tend to drift downhill. If you have to ride across a gentle slope, aim slightly uphill and keep your lower leg firmly on the girth.

If you need to cross steep ground, ride straight up or down it and look for a flatter route across that will be easier for your pony to tackle.

If you have to jump a fence on the side of a hill, take an uphill approach.

RIDING DOWNHILL

It is harder for your pony to balance when going downhill, as his hindquarters are above him. He will tend to take longer strides which makes it easy for him to pick up speed. You need to stay in a safe, upright position. Let your pony stretch his neck out, but don't let him fall forward.

On very steep slopes your pony will take lots of shorter steps. Stay still and straight and make sure he doesn't get out of control.

Trotting downhill
- Only trot down gentle slopes.
- Avoid trotting downhill if the ground is hard.
- Make sure you are in complete control.
- Keep a rising trot but try not to bump down hard in the saddle.

Keep your heels down, otherwise your feet may slide through the stirrups, as this rider's have.

Walk slowly down a steep slope, staying calm and supple, so that you can go with your pony's movement.

ADDING STUDS TO YOUR PONY'S SHOES

Studs can be useful on steep terrain or in difficult ground conditions. If you want to use them, you have to ask your farrier to make holes for them in your pony's shoes.

This is usually done on the outside of the shoes. When not using studs, pack the holes with oiled cotton to stop them from filling with dirt. Here's how to put one in:

Use a farrier's nail.

Remove the cotton from the stud hole and clean it out.

Stud tap

Use a stud tap to clear the thread inside the hole.

Holding your pony's foot firmly, screw in the stud.

Tighten stud, using the tap's other end or a crescent wrench.

GETTING FIT

Both pony and rider need to be fit for any type of competition, but cross-country in particular will test your stamina to the full. In order to avoid injury, it is important to start training slowly and gradually build up to faster speeds. You will need to build up your pony's food too.

PLANNING YOUR TRAINING

It takes about eight weeks to get a pony fit for a preliminary cross-country competition. The first four weeks will be slow work at walk and trot. The next four will be longer, faster hacks and schooling work. The table below shows how to build up your work over an eight-week period and the list on the right includes a few other points you need to consider when planning your own program.

Points to consider

- Before you start, get your pony shod, make sure his vaccinations are up to date and have his teeth checked.

- If your pony has been out of work, allow longer for the early stages.
- If you have already been competing and attending shows or events, you can do less slow work and concentrate on the faster work right away.
- Work your pony six days a week and let him have one day a week off.

- Vary the work as much as possible. From week five try for two long, slow hacks, two schooling sessions and two sessions of faster work each week.
- Follow a day of fast work with a day off or a long, slow hack.

EIGHT-WEEK PROGRAM		
Week	Hacking	Schooling
1	½ – 1hour walk	
2	1 – 1½ hour walk	
3	Add trots	
4	Add gentle hillwork	
5	Add canters	From week 5 add basic schooling at walk and trot.
6	Increase canters	Work at canter Add trotting poles
7	Longer, steeper hills Add small jumps	Include gridwork
8	Long, steady canters Short gallops	More gridwork

SLOW WORK ON ROADS AND TRACKS

To begin with, simply walk your pony out on firm, flat ground. Quiet roads and tracks are ideal. This helps strengthen the bones, tendons and ligaments in his legs, which will help prevent lameness later on.

Always encourage your pony to walk energetically so that his muscles are toned up too. Introduce trotting and then hillwork a little at a time.

On firm, flat ground, boots help to protect your pony's legs. On roads he should wear knee boots too.

Your pony's legs
Check the ligaments, tendons, and splint bone for heat or swelling after work (see page 31 to find out how to do this).

Splint bone

Tendon

Canon bone

Ligaments

SCHOOLING FOR RHYTHM AND BALANCE

Exercises with turns and circles loosen your pony up and make him supple.

After about four weeks of gentle hacking, start schooling your pony in walk and trot. This will improve his balance and rhythm as well as teaching him to be obedient.

When you are ready to make your pony work a little harder, add some exercises over trotting poles and small cross poles. Start schooling in canter as well as walk and trot.

As your pony's fitness improves, try some gridwork (jumping down a line of small fences). This is excellent jump training and will help make your pony supple.

BUILDING UP SPEED

A lot of cross-country is ridden at a canter or gallop, so it is important to practice these gaits. Build up to them gradually so as to avoid any unnecessary strains.

From week five you can start cantering on your hacks. Start with occasional, short canters and build up to longer, more frequent ones. Make sure your pony stays obedient and that you stay in full control. By the end of the seventh week you should be ready for a short gallop.

When you're out hacking, look out for ditches, hedges or logs that you could use as practice jumps. Always check the takeoff and landing first.

A good gallop is fun for you and your pony, but keep it short and stay in control.

CHECKING PULSE AND RESPIRATION

As you gradually increase the amount of fast work you do, you need to keep a check on your pony's condition by taking his pulse and respiration after exercise, as shown in the pictures on the right.

After a canter your pony should puff slightly, but not be completely out of breath. After about ten minutes his pulse and respiration should have returned to normal. If they haven't, he is working too hard and you need to build up to fast work more gradually.

Pulse
A pony's normal pulse rate (the number of times his heart beats each minute) should be 36 to 42. You can feel his pulse under his jaw or just above his eye.

Respiration
His normal respiration rate (the number of breaths he takes each minute) is 8 to 12. To count them, watch his flanks go in and out, or put your hand near his nose.

FOOD FOR FITNESS

As you increase your pony's work, you will need to feed him less bulk food and more concentrates. Be careful not to give too much rich food too quickly though, as this can lead to pains in his tummy or cramps. Watch your own pony carefully. Some ponies put on weight very easily. Others lose it fast. A lively pony will be easier to manage if fed more hay, while a lazy one may benefit from more oats.

Bulk food, such as hay and grass, is what fills a pony up and keeps his digestion working.

Concentrates, such as pellets or sweet feed, give a pony extra energy.

The table below shows how the food of a 14hh pony, eating a total of about 9kg (20lbs) of food a day, may change over an eight-week fitness program.

Week	Bulk food	Concentrates
1	8.6kg (19lbs)	450g (1lb)
2	8.2kg (18lbs)	900g (2lbs)
3	7.7kg (17lbs)	1.4kg (3lbs)
4	7.3kg (16lbs)	1.8kg (4lbs)
5	6.8kg (15lbs)	2.3kg (5lbs)
6	6.4kg (14lbs)	2.7kg (6lbs)
7	5.9kg (13lbs)	3.2kg (7lbs)
8	5.4kg (12lbs)	3.6kg (8lbs)

IMPROVING YOUR FITNESS

Exercises without stirrups make you work harder and improve your fitness.

Push-ups strengthen your upper body, which is useful if you have a strong pony.

It is just as important for you to be fit as it is for your pony. Cross-country riding can be exhausting and you don't want to be the one to let your pony down. If you ride every day, you will get pretty fit anyway.

If you are unable to ride out every day, plan some other form of exercise. Skipping, jogging, swimming, or even energetic tasks such as sweeping the stables, will improve your fitness.

Add some exercises to help keep you supple, such as touching your toes or doing sit-ups. Ask a gym teacher to show you how to do these exercises correctly, so that you do not damage your muscles.

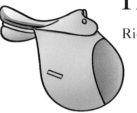

TACK AND EQUIPMENT

Riding at speed and jumping put more stress on your tack than normal, so it is important to have good quality equipment. Check it regularly and keep it clean and supple. Both you and your pony will need protective clothing too, to guard against knocks and falls.

YOUR PONY'S TACK

A general purpose saddle is fine for cross-country. Use a comfortable saddle pad, made of natural fibers, under it. Avoid new tack, which can be uncomfortable, but check all used tack for wear and tear. Choose stainless steel bits and stirrups, and rubber reins for a better grip. For additional safety or better control, you may want to use some of the items shown below. However, only use this stronger tack if it is really necessary and always try it out before a competition.

Nosebands

Flash *Drop* *Figure eight*

Flash, drop and figure eight nosebands all have straps that fasten behind the chin. This stops your pony from opening his mouth to avoid the pressure of the bit, giving you more control.

Bits

Snaffle – a very gentle bit

Dr. Bristol – puts more pressure on the tongue

Kimblewick – a much stronger type of bit

A change of bit can help control a strong pony, but the wrong one can do more damage than good. Try several with the advice of your instructor if you feel the need to change.

Martingales

A running martingale is the most popular type, but it must be expertly fitted.

A martingale stops a pony from throwing his head up and causing you to lose control. It also provides you with a neckstrap to grab when your pony takes a particularly sudden or large leap.

Girths and overgirths

Overgirth
Girths

One of the worst things that can happen to your tack on cross-country is a girth breaking. This is why top riders use two webbing girths as well as an over-girth, which fastens all the way around the saddle.

Breastplates

Breastplate

A breastplate is sometimes used to help keep the saddle in place and stop it from slipping backward on steep ground. It must be loosely fitted so that it does not restrict your pony's chest as he jumps.

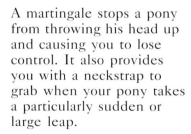

WHAT YOU SHOULD WEAR

Cross-country dress used to be hunting attire (tweeds and black hat) but since safety vests and hard hats have become obligatory, silks and sweatshirts are more common. You can match them with saddle pads and bandages, but check with your instructor that all of your equipment meets current safety standards.

A firmly-tied stock can give your neck extra support.

Shirts or sweaters need long sleeves to protect your arms.

Your hard hat must have chin straps and meet safety standards.

A bright cover over your hard hat is a colorful addition to your outfit.

Safety vests can be worn over or under sweatshirts but they must meet safety standards.

Spurs can be useful for a balking or lazy pony but are not always allowed. Check with the organizers first.

String gloves give the best grip. Leather can be slippery when wet.

Choose long or short boots with smooth soles, pointed toes and small heels.

Breeches or jodhpurs need extra protection and grip inside the knees.

A short crop can be useful as an extra aid at difficult fences.

PROTECTING YOUR PONY'S LEGS

Your pony's heels and legs can get battered and bruised across country so you need to protect them with boots or bandages. There's a wide range available, but the main areas that need protection are the front and back of the legs and around the fetlock joints. Leather boots are a good choice, as they are easy to put on and don't absorb water. Avoid materials which soak up water.

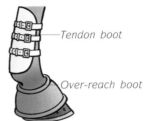

Tendon boot

Over-reach boot

Boots should be lightweight, close-fitting and securely fastened. Make sure they do not impede circulation.

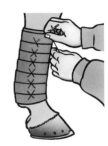

Bandages must be expertly fitted and sewn in place over quilts, so that there's no risk of them coming undone.

CROSS-COUNTRY FENCES

There's a huge variety of cross-country fences. Some of the most common are described on the next few pages. The one feature they all have in common, and which makes them different from show jumps, is that they are nearly always solid so they won't fall over if knocked.

JUMPING YOUR FIRST SOLID FENCES

Many riders find the thought of a solid fence quite scary. In fact, a solid fence is easier for a pony to see, which means he judges the takeoff better and is likely to make a bolder leap. Your position and technique for cross-country fences is much the same as for schooling fences, though the pace may be a little faster.

When starting out, choose a fence on flat ground, with a good takeoff and landing. Low sleepers, a wide log or small log pile are all solid but easy fences to start over.

For practice jumping on hills or difficult ground, first try a small hedge. It's less dangerous if you do make a mistake. Below are a few general points to remember.

Jumping tips
● Keep a straight, controlled approach.
● As you take off, bend forward from the hips not the waist.
● Let your hands move forward with the pony's neck so that you don't pull him in the mouth.
● Keep your lower legs straight. If they swing back, you will tip forward; if they go forward, you will fall back.
● Keep your heels down and your lower legs close to your pony's sides, ready to urge on if he hesitates.
● Look straight ahead, don't lean to one side.
● As soon as you land, get back into position, ready for the next fence.

A solid tree trunk is a good introduction to cross-country fences.

SPREAD FENCES

Spreads are wide fences which need to be approached at a stronger pace. Balance is still more important than speed, but encouraging your pony to lengthen his stride will help him to clear a spread fence.

Tires

Tiger trap

Round or triangular shaped spreads, such as tires, tiger traps or a log pile, are the easiest to jump.

Table

Parallel bars

Square shapes, such as a table or parallel bars, need a more careful approach in case your pony needs to fit in an extra stride before takeoff.

Chair

Triple bar

Spreads that start low and get higher, such as a triple bar, or chair, are easier than the squarer shapes, but you will need to take off closer to the fence.

Spread fences can seem huge, but are often an easier shape for a pony to jump than an upright.

UPRIGHT FENCES

Upright fences may look smaller than spreads, but they are often harder for a pony to judge. If he takes off too late he may hit the fence with his front legs. If he takes off too early he may catch it with his hind legs. Approach steadily so that he has time to see the fence and judge the takeoff point.

For an upright fence, your pony's hocks need to be well engaged (tucked in underneath him), so that he has the power to push off and clear the height.

Hock

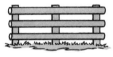
Post and rails

Style

Narrow uprights, such as a style, need a very straight, controlled approach.

Stone wall

Gate

Bullfinch

Palisade

A bullfinch may look higher than other upright fences, but your pony can brush his legs through the top part. Inexperienced ponies may try to jump the full height.

DITCHES

Ditches of all sizes, shapes and forms are a common cross-country obstacle. You will come across them on their own or as part of another fence. They are not difficult to jump, but many ponies and riders find them scary. Practicing over plenty of small, simple ditches will help both of you to build up confidence.

NATURAL DITCHES

Most ponies find natural ditches less scary than man-made ones, so practicing back and forth over a small natural ditch is a good way to build up confidence. Always check the takeoff and landing. If it is slippery or muddy, approach with extra caution.

Bear in mind that your pony won't see a ditch until he gets quite close, so approach slowly enough for him to realize what he has to jump, but fast enough for him to clear the ditch easily. The wider the ditch, the longer his stride needs to be.

A pony can jump a small ditch from a standstill, so if your pony stops, try urging him on rather than turning around to approach again. Be ready for a large leap.

Ponies can easily take a small ditch in their stride, but they often jump large, like this one, who has unseated his rider.

TACKLING A COFFIN

A coffin is a difficult three-part combination fence. It includes a fence in, a ditch (often with a slope down into it) and a fence out.

To jump it successfully, you need to approach at a steady pace and keep impulsion all the way through.

Approach at a steady, bouncy canter.

If you jump the first part too fast, your pony might land too close to, or even in the ditch.

Be ready to urge your pony on in case he spooks at the ditch.

FENCES WITH A DITCH

Ditch away

When there is a ditch behind a fence (a ditch away), your pony will not know it is there. Approach at a strong pace so that your pony jumps out boldly and clears the ditch.

Open ditch

A ditch in front of a fence is called an open ditch. It can be quite helpful as it gives a guideline for takeoff, which encourages your pony to make a bold leap.

Trakhener

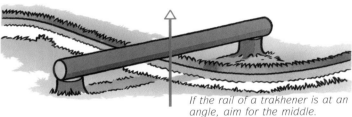

If the rail of a trakhener is at an angle, aim for the middle.

A ditch with a rail over it is called a trakhener. The rail makes your pony jump higher and wider.

Approach at a steady pace and be ready to urge your pony on if he suddenly sees the ditch and spooks.

Never look down into a ditch. Your pony will be able to sense your fear.

Sit back in the saddle as soon as you land, in order to keep a safe position and maintain impulsion.

There is usually room for one, or sometimes two strides between each part of the fence.

Keeping a good, straight line all the way through the coffin will help ensure that you have an accurate approach at the last fence.

WATER

Most ponies are naturally frightened of water, and yet, with training, many come to love it. Cross-country events usually include some kind of water obstacle, so it is worth getting your pony used to water if you want to compete.

WATER TRAINING

Whenever you are out hacking, look for opportunities to introduce your pony to water. On a rainy day there will be lots of puddles which are perfect to splash through.

Shallow streams are good, but make sure the bottom is firm. If your pony starts sinking into mud or tripping on rocks, he will be even more nervous.

Remember that your pony does not know how deep the water is. He has to trust you. A very nervous pony will often be happier following another pony. Let them stand in the water together and splash around so that they get the feel of it.

Once your pony is confident about walking and paddling in water, try trotting him through. Then you are ready to try a jump in or out of water (see opposite).

Take your pony through as many different water obstacles as possible, so that he is confident with all water, not just familiar spots. Remember that most ponies find man-made water obstacles more spooky than natural ones.

Allowing ponies to splash around together teaches them that water can be fun, not frightening. Once they have overcome their fear, they will begin to enjoy trotting and jumping in water.

JUMPING OUT OF WATER

Once your pony will trot through water confidently, try a small jump on the way out. At first, position the jump a stride away from the water, so that your pony can take off from dry land.

Then move the jump closer so that he has to take off from the water. Approach at a strong trot and keep urging him on so that he has enough impulsion to jump. The drag of the water will slow him down.

Start with the jump a stride away from the water.

Then move the jump so that you take off from the water.

JUMPING INTO WATER

As with the jump out, start with the fence a stride away from the water, so that your pony can land on dry ground. Keep it small so that if your pony stops, you can encourage him to step over it rather than turning away. Once confident over this, try a small drop directly into water. (For more about drop fences see page 21.)

For larger drops or fences you will need to approach in a trot or gentle canter, but keep it slow and steady so that your pony can drop gently into the water.

Landing in water will slow your pony down suddenly, so if you approach too fast you might both be caught unprepared.

TACKLING A FENCE IN WATER

Water slows your pony right down, so jumping a fence in water requires a lot of effort. It is also hard for your pony to judge how high to jump, so you need to be ready to urge him on strongly. This means it is essential for you to get your balance back, after a jump into water.

STEPS, BANKS AND DROPS

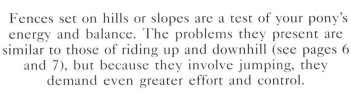

Fences set on hills or slopes are a test of your pony's energy and balance. The problems they present are similar to those of riding up and downhill (see pages 6 and 7), but because they involve jumping, they demand even greater effort and control.

STEPS UP OR DOWN

Approach steps in the same way as normal upright fences – not too fast, but with plenty of impulsion. Let your pony jump up a single small step at first so he gets used to landing on higher ground. The more steps there are, the more impulsion you need. Urge him on all the way up.

Jumping down a step is more difficult for your pony, but he needs very little impulsion. Start over one small step, and if he is nervous, let him stand at the top and look down. Never turn away or he will learn to refuse. If necessary, take a lead from another pony. Be ready for a huge leap when he does go, and have a neckstrap to hold onto, or grab a piece of mane so you don't pull his mouth. As he gains confidence he will jump smaller.

Once your pony jumps confidently down a single step, try him over a series. Always approach slowly.

BANKS

Banks are tackled in a similar way to steps. Sit slightly forward for the jump up, but then adopt an upright seat on top of the bank, ready for the jump down.

A bank is a step up... followed by a step down.

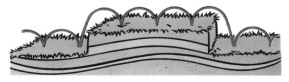

SUNKEN ROAD

A sunken road is like an upside-down bank. Approach in a steady, bouncy canter and concentrate on keeping good balance all the way through.

A sunken road is a step down... followed by a step up.

DROP FENCES

A drop fence is one where the landing is lower than takeoff. Your pony may not know this when he takes off, so you must keep good balance and not interfere. The landing is the hard part. Sit slightly back and keep your lower leg forward to help you balance. Above all, be ready to slip your reins (see bottom of this page) so that you do not jab your pony in the mouth. Keep a controlled approach, but increase the stride, so that your pony jumps out over the drop rather than landing in it.

Sit upright, or slightly back for landing.

If your approach is fast and the stride long, your pony will land a long way from the fence.

If your approach is slow and the stride short, your pony will land too close to the fence.

A steady approach with a medium-length stride will result in a more comfortable landing.

This rider has slipped her reins to let her pony have his head. Her lower legs are well forward and her heels down, giving her a secure position for landing.

SLIPPING YOUR REINS

Your pony uses his head and neck for balance, so when jumping downhill he must be able to stretch his neck out. But because you need to sit up or even slightly back in order to keep your balance, the only way to let him have his neck, is to allow the reins to slip through your hands. You recover them like this:

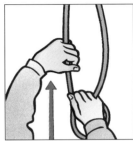

As your pony stretches his neck, open your fingers to let the reins slip through your hands.

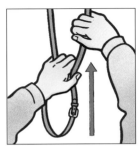

To pick up contact, put both reins into your right hand and slide your left hand down the left rein.

Then hold both reins in your left hand and slide your right hand down the right rein.

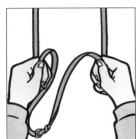

Your reins should now be the correct length to take back control and continue your ride.

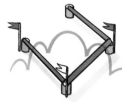

COMBINATION FENCES

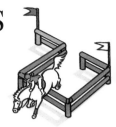

A combination fence is one where you have to tackle two or more jumps in a row. Most cross-country courses include a few. They vary from a simple jump in and out, to a more complex system of fences where you must choose your own route through. Before tackling any combination, you need to figure out how many strides your pony will take between each jump.

JUDGING YOUR PONY'S STRIDE

Set up schooling fences at home to figure out how many of your strides are equal to one of your pony's. Three short strides are often about equal to one pony stride, but it is best to work it out for yourself as it will depend on the size of both you and your pony. You need to include a couple of your strides for your pony's takeoff and landing strides too (see the diagrams below). When you come across a combination, pace out the distance between the fences. If you manage only nine strides between the fences, try to steady your pony so that he can put in two shorter strides. If you manage eight, urge him on to take one longer stride.

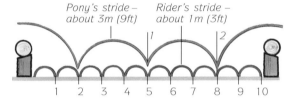

Here, ten rider's strides equal two pony strides.

Include a couple of strides for the pony's takeoff and landing.

Pony's stride – about 3m (9ft)   Rider's stride – about 1m (3ft)

1   2   3   4   5   6   7   8   9   10

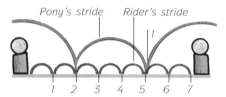

Here, seven rider's strides equal one pony stride.

Pony's stride   Rider's stride

1   2   3   4   5   6   7

A SIMPLE IN AND OUT

Before tackling two jumps in a row, figure out how many strides you think your pony will take between them (see above). There may be room for several, but the fewer there are, the more accurate you must be in figuring out the number of strides. Steady your pony on the approach, so that he has time to see the jump, and keep him straight, so that he cannot run out at the second one.

This in and out allows room for two short strides, so the rider has been careful to approach steadily.

She concentrates on keeping her pony straight through the middle, steadying him slightly...

...and then urges him on to make sure they clear the second part of the in and out easily.

BOUNCE FENCES

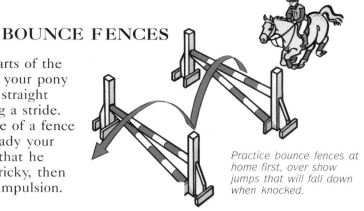

In a bounce fence, the two parts of the combination are so close that your pony has to jump in and "bounce" straight back out again, without taking a stride. It is best to approach this type of a fence in a short, bouncy canter. Steady your pony several strides away so that he knows to expect something tricky, then urge him on, keeping lots of impulsion.

Practice bounce fences at home first, over show jumps that will fall down when knocked.

CHOOSING YOUR ROUTE

When you are given a choice of routes through a combination, there is usually a slower, easier one and a faster, more difficult one. As long as you remember to keep the red flag on the right and the white flag on the left, you can choose the route that suits you best.

The diagrams below show some examples of the types of combination fences you might encounter in a cross-country competition.

Tight turns
Some combination fences involve jumping in one way, and then turning and jumping out in a different direction. This involves good control and a much slower approach.

─── This shows the fastest, hardest route.

─── This shows the slowest, easiest route.

─── This shows an intermediate route.

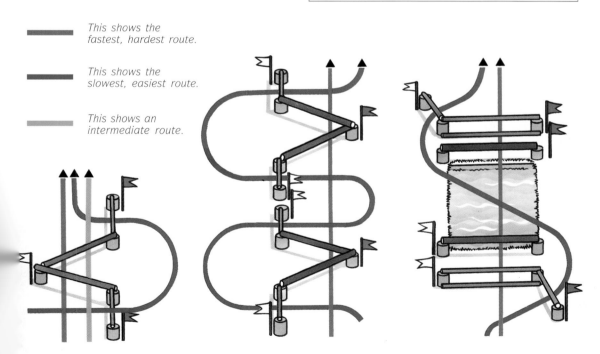

CORNERS AND ARROWHEADS

Corners and arrowheads require very accurate riding, and, because of this, they are often part of the fast but difficult option in a combination fence. It's a good idea to practice these jumps at home first, using blocks and poles that will fall down if things go wrong.

CORNERS

This rider has ridden a very accurate line close to the flag so that her horse jumps the narrowest part of this large corner fence.

On cross-country courses, a corner is usually part of an angled rails fence which offers several possible routes. If your pony is jumping well, and you can ride accurately, it's a good option to take.

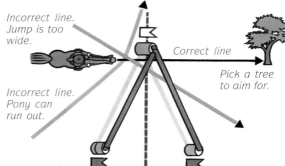

Incorrect line. Jump is too wide.

Correct line

Pick a tree to aim for.

Incorrect line. Pony can run out.

It's important to get the angle of your approach right. If you aim straight at the front rail, the jump becomes very wide. If you aim straight at the back one, your pony may run out. Imagine a line cutting the corner in two (like the dotted one in the diagram above) and ride straight at that. Pick a landmark in the distance to help you aim straight. See opposite for more tips on riding a straight line.

PRACTICING CORNERS

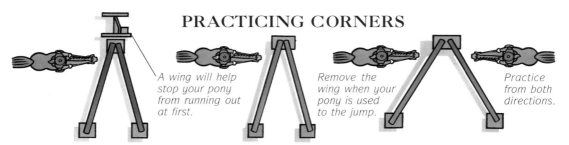

A wing will help stop your pony from running out at first.

Remove the wing when your pony is used to the jump.

Practice from both directions.

Use blocks and poles to build a narrow corner at first. If necessary, add a wing to help guide your pony into the fence. Once your pony is used to the jump, take the wing away. Then gradually widen the angle of the corner. Practice jumping the corner from both directions so that your pony doesn't become one-sided.

TACKLING ARROWHEADS

An arrowhead is a difficult fence and therefore often the hardest option in a combination fence. You could be expected to jump either into the arrow or against the point (see the diagram below).

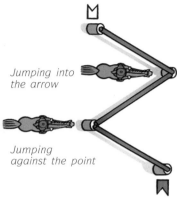

Jumping into the arrow

Jumping against the point

This rider has made a good straight approach right against the point of the arrowhead and as a result is making a very successful jump.

With either approach, the arrowhead requires accurate riding and a very straight approach. Most ponies will try and jump to one side, which can be disastrous with a solid fence, so you should practice this at home first.

Tips for keeping straight

- Look straight ahead.
- Keep both legs firmly against your pony's sides.
- Keep an even contact with the reins.
- Approach slowly in a short, bouncy canter so that you have plenty of control to direct your pony to the center of the jump.

PRACTICING ARROWHEADS

Leave a gap.

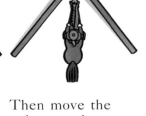

Begin by leaning two poles on a single rail, as shown here. Keep your pony very straight and aim right for the middle.

Then move the poles together so that they narrow to a point. Be very strict about making your pony jump the point.

Take the horizontal pole away and balance the other two on a block or straw bale. You can gradually make the V narrower.

Once your pony jumps this well, try approaching from the other side. This is harder because the poles no longer act as wings.

25

OTHER OBSTACLES

Cross-country courses vary from area to area and each has its own unique jumps, so you'll often have to tackle something completely new. These pages deal with some other common obstacles, such as riding through wooded areas and opening and closing gates. Last, but not least, is the ordeal of the starting gate for competition riders.

RIDING THROUGH WOODS

Riding through wooded areas brings new obstacles, such as overhanging branches or changing light conditions (see below).

Unless you live in an area of very open countryside, you are likely to be riding through woods at some point. This usually means following rugged tracks or narrow paths, and dealing with tight turns and overhanging branches.

Ground conditions in woods are often rougher than in the open, and you will need to keep an eye open for tree roots and other hazards.

At events you need good control and accurate riding in order to be able to tackle these areas at a sensible speed.

Watch out for turns off a main track onto a smaller path as this is a real test of control, particularly just before or after a jump.

CHANGING LIGHT CONDITIONS

Wooded areas also mean changes in the light. This can make a simple fence into or out of the woods look far harder to your pony than it actually is.

Approach this type of fence with lots of impulsion, but not too fast, so that your pony's eyes have time to adjust. Be ready to urge him on if he hesitates.

Fences in partial shade, such as those on the edge of the woods, can also cause problems. A pony may shy away from the darkness, and therefore run out.

HOW TO OPEN AND CLOSE A GATE

Opening and closing a gate while mounted can be tricky, but it is an essential skill for all types of cross-country riding, so it is worth practicing. An obedient pony makes it much easier. A gate is sometimes included as part of a hunter trial course too, where you might be judged on style or speed.

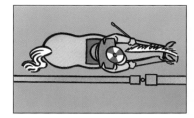

1. Ride alongside the gate and bring your pony to a halt when his head is just past the catch.

2. Put the reins and crop in your outside hand, so that you can use the other one to undo the catch.

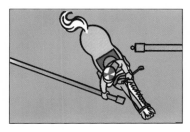

3. Push the gate open and walk your pony through. Keep hold of the gate, if possible, while you do this.

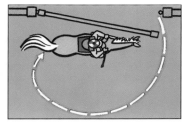

4. Turn your pony around, keeping close to the outside of the gate, so that it doesn't swing wide open.

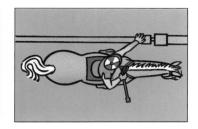

5. Put the reins and the crop into your other hand, push the gate closed, and then fasten the catch.

COPING WITH THE START IN COMPETITIONS

At the start of most competitions you wait in a small, fenced-off area called the start box. The starter counts you down and as soon as he or she says "Go!" you must head toward the first fence.

Some ponies get nervous and excited while waiting; others are reluctant to set off and leave "home". Make sure your pony is warmed up before you go to the start and then keep him walking around calmly until you are called into the start box.

Avoid going into the box too early if your pony is excited, and when you do go in, face the back. A calm pony can go in earlier and face the start. If he is reluctant to set off, give him a tap with the crop.

Try to make a good, strong start from the box.

27

ENTERING AN EVENT

One of the best chances you will get to ride over a course of cross-country fences is by taking part in a local event, such as hunter trials. These are usually organized by the local hunt or Pony Club. You can find out about them from saddlers, riding schools, Pony Clubs and local newspapers.

HOW TO ENTER AN EVENT

Hunter trials often include pairs classes which are fun to do with a friend and give you the chance to follow another pony around a course.

Send off for a schedule and check the conditions of each class. They are usually divided according to the experience of the rider and pony or height of the jumps. Only enter one or two classes, making sure they are the most suitable.

Checklist
- Send off for schedule.
- Choose class or classes, checking rules carefully.
- Send back entry form and fee by closing date (with a stamped addressed envelope, if requested).
- Find out if you are to be given a start time before the day. If so, make a note of when to call for it.

WHAT TO DO ON THE BIG DAY

If you plan to walk the course the same day, you will need to arrive at least two hours before the start. Try to park on flat ground so that your pony is as comfortable as possible while he is waiting.

Visit the secretary's tent first to collect your number and the course map. Check whether things are running on time and find out whether you need to put your name down for the start or whether you have already been given a starting time.

Study the course map and check the details of your class carefully.

WALKING THE COURSE

Walking the course is the one chance you get to study the jumps up close and learn the route you are going to take. The course may be open the day before. Don't forget to wear comfortable shoes or rubber boots if there's water to wade through.

Pick up a course map, or study the one at the secretary's tent before you start walking.

Course checklist

- Study each takeoff and landing. Muddy ones are likely to get worse during the day, so plan an alternative approach.
- Check fence numbers. Each class uses a different color, so ensure you know which is for your class.

- Look out for turning flags – two red and white ones you have to go through; a single red you must keep to your right.
- Look at any fence with options. Plan your best route plus a second in case the first goes wrong.
- At each fence, choose a line that will bring you in straight. Try to find a landmark to help.
- Walk the exact route you plan to ride.
- Look for any things that your pony might find spooky, such as hidden officials.

- Jot down notes on your map as you go. You can read through them just before you set off.
- If time, go back to the course to watch other competitors ride it.
- Check where the finish flags are and make sure you ride through them.

WARMING UP

Your pony needs a gentle 15-20 minute warm-up before setting off on the course. Pop over the practice jump a couple of times – no more, or your pony may get bored before he starts. If you have to wait at the start, walk around at a brisk pace. Have a short trot and canter just before you set off to ensure your pony is alert.

AFTER AN EVENT

Riding a cross-country course is exhausting work for your pony as well as for you. It is very important that you take good care of him immediately after finishing the course and over the next few days in order to prevent him from becoming stiff, cold or even lame.

WHEN YOU FINISH THE COURSE

1. When you finish the course your pony is likely to be hot and breathing quite fast. Pull up slowly, so that he doesn't stumble.

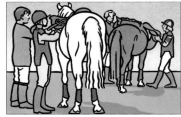

2. Come back to a steady walk and then halt and dismount. Now you can loosen the girth and run up the stirrups.

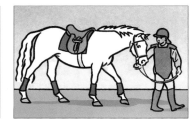

3. Walk him around until he has cooled off and caught his breath. It should take about ten minutes (see page 10).

4. Once back at the trailer, remove his saddle and check him over carefully, paying particular attention to his legs (see opposite).

5. On a warm day, sponge his neck and saddle patch with cold water. Otherwise just use a sweat scraper to remove the sweat.

Offer several small drinks rather than one long one.

6. Put on a sweat sheet and continue walking him around until he is cool. When he has stopped puffing, offer him a drink.

7. Remove bandages, boots or studs. Rub his legs with a towel to dry them and get the circulation going. If it is warm, wash them.

8. If it is a cold day, add an extra blanket on top of the sweat sheet. Now you can give him a little hay and leave him to rest.

9. When you have taken care of your pony, you can get some food for yourself and return your number to the secretary's tent.

GETTING HOME

Make sure your pony is blanketed and warm for the journey home from the competition. Put shipping bandages on to protect his legs.

As soon as you get home after an event, walk your pony around again to prevent him from getting stiff before putting him in the stall. Check his legs again, put on his night blankets and give him a small feeding. Make sure he has plenty of fresh water.

If he lives at pasture and it's cold, add a turn-out blanket. Check him once more before you go to bed.

THE NEXT DAY

Check again for signs of injury. Pick out his feet and check his shoes. Then turn him out in the field for an hour or two. When you bring him in, groom him, making sure to remove any dry sweat. Let him have a day off and two easier working days before you jump him again. Watch for signs of poor health and feed less concentrates and more bulk when he's not working.

Health checklist
- Is he behaving normally?
- Are his eyes bright?
- Does his coat look shiny?
- Does he seem cheerful and lively?
- Is he eating well?
- Do his droppings look the same as usual and are they as frequent?

CHECKING AND CARING FOR THE LEGS

Your pony's legs can easily get injured across country. After work, run your hand down each leg carefully, checking for any cuts, heat or swelling.

Treating cuts
Wash cuts gently and hose them with cold water. If they are minor, apply a little antiseptic cream or spray. If more serious, just hose them and call the vet in case your pony needs stitches, antibiotics or a tetanus booster.

Holding a stream of cold water over your pony's legs is the best way to treat any cuts, bruises or swelling.

Stand near the girth area when you hose your pony's legs, in case he kicks out.

Heat and swelling
Heat and swelling may just mean some bruising or it could be a symptom of something more severe, such as a strained tendon. To treat heat and swelling, hose the affected area with cold water for about 20 minutes three or four times a day. Holding an ice pack on the area also helps (a bag of frozen peas is excellent). If the swelling persists, or if your pony is lame too, you should call the vet.

INDEX

With thanks to: Robin Dumas, Rosamund Green Farm, Shepton Mallet;
Katherine Woolmer and Pepe, Rose Castle and Harry, Flossy Castle and Jigtime;
Didi and Michael Kingscote, Lydeard Farm, Broomfield, Bridgwater.